*My dedication is to you, in honor of the
great gifts you bring to our world!*

Thank you for who you are!

Brian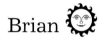

This is a story about you and me, but for the protection of us... Hmmm, let me see... I have it... here we go...

4

Our story begins as we look in on two ant families that came from different colonies. They lived very close to one another. The Blacks were beautiful in color, one-half black, and one-half blue. Their colors created a wonderful hue. The Reds were also beautiful in color, one-half red, and one-half blue. Their colors also created a wonderful hue.

And so, we begin!

"I can't stand the Reds," cried Mr. Black.

"I know what you mean," replied his wife from the crack.
"They have been our enemies since who knows when. When
our kids learn to hate them, their lives will be better then!"

"Yes," replied Mr. Black. "I know what we must do; we must teach our children to hate the Reds, and to only like the Black and Blue."

Just down the street from the Blacks lived the Reds. It was early morning as they woke from their beds. "Ho hum," yawned Mr. Red, as he focused the thoughts that ran through his head. "Hmmm," he said to his wife, "I hate the Blacks, and I'll hate them for life!"

"I know what you mean," replied Mrs. Red, "I can't stand them either!" she said shaking her head. "They have been our enemies since who knows when. When our kids learn to hate them, their lives will be better then! I know what we must do; we must teach our children to hate the Blacks, and to only like the Red and Blue."

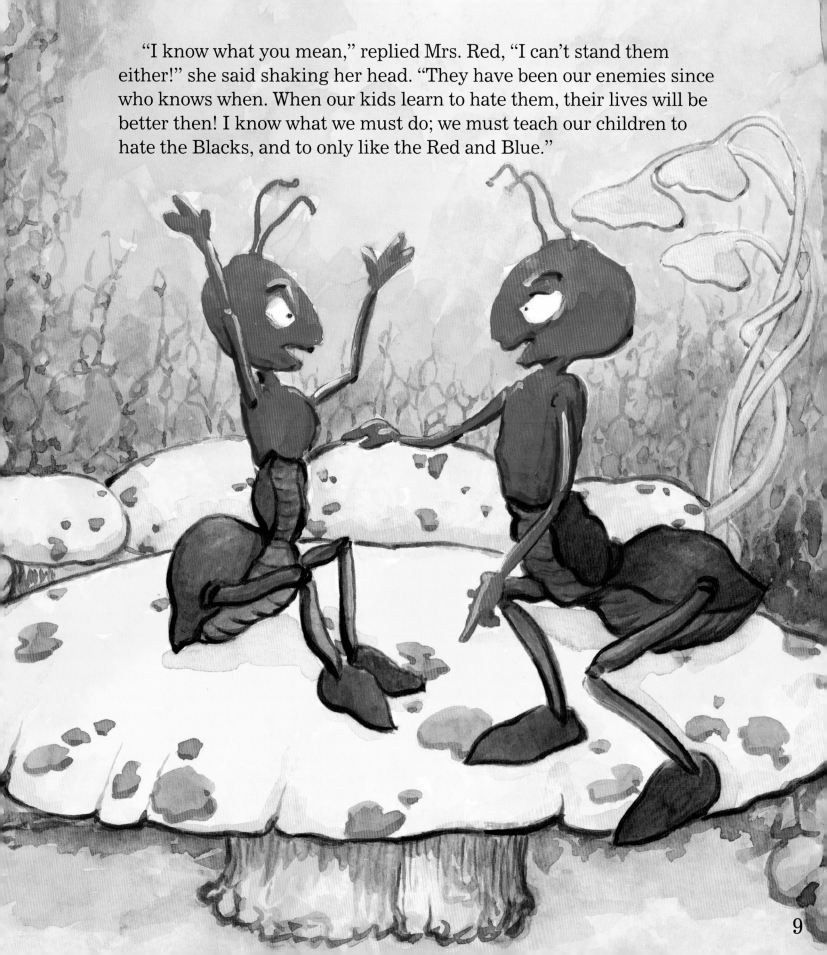

9

Such was the talk at the ant houses that day,
and it usually took place in the very same way.

Now for you and me, it is easy to see, that the Blacks and the Reds were acting just like humans. Sometimes we hold beliefs about others, which may have been passed down from our fathers and mothers. We think our beliefs to be correct and true. But, we only consider the world, through our limited view. We act out of fear, and believe our conscious to be clear. That doesn't mean that we are right, and it gives us no justification to fight!

11

Back at the Black residence, the two children were just waking up. Cheri and Matt were sister and brother, and the nice thing about them is, they liked one another.

Wherever they were, they would laugh and play; it was always the same for each new day. They found joy in all they did. They had not yet been taught that the Reds were forbid. For them, their world was simple and whole, fun and joy was their only goal.

13

Just down the street at the Red residence, the two children were already eating their breakfast toast. They sure loved life, their parents would boast.

Ron and Sal were twins from the start, and since they were born, they had never been apart. Wherever they were, they would laugh and play; it was always the same for each new day. They found joy in all they did. They had not yet been taught that the Blacks were forbid. For them their world was simple and whole, fun and joy was their only goal.

For the Red and the Black parents, the children's future happiness was their key. The joy their children felt in the moment was just too hard for them to see. Thus, feeling there was no time to waste; they started teaching their children, with quite a rushed pace.

"You must learn to hate the Blacks," was the Red parents' call.

"You must learn to hate the Reds," came the Black parents' squall.

Now let's stop the story for a moment or two, there are a few things about humans that I would like to explain to you.

Sometimes humans teach us things, that aren't always true.
Now, they don't do that on purpose, to me and to you. They teach
the things that they were taught, when they were young like us...
things that they believe are true, so they teach without a fuss.
Now many times the things they teach are absolutely right,
sometimes though, they teach us things that cause us to fight.

For all parents, their children's happiness is the key. That comes directly from the love they have, which is unconditional for you and me. Wanting to protect us, and teaching from their fear, they sometimes teach a twisted truth, which to us may seem unclear. That doesn't make them right or wrong... only unaware. They would never teach to hurt us, because they really care!

Now let's get back to our story...

19

Far away from the Black and Red colonies lived another ant colony, the Blues. The Blues were beautiful in color, one-quarter black, one-quarter red, and one-half blue. Their colors created a wonderful hue.

The Blue's were a happy family of four; they lived in the east, by the old seashore. Swan and Terry were sister and brother; they loved everyone, just like their father and mother. Acceptance of all was what they learned from the start. It was a belief that their parents held, deep in their heart.

One day, as Terry and Swan played by the shore, they saw a boat, and decided to explore. They climbed up the anchor to the very top, and when they jumped inside the boat, they started screaming, "Stop!" The boat had set sail, which caused both Blues, to scream and wail. "Let us off," was the cry, as the crew just continued to wave goodbye.

The boat had moved well away from the dock, for Terry and Swan, it was a terrible shock! They were on their way to who knows where. Their overriding feeling was one of despair. The only good news, if there was any to be had, is that they were together, although they were sad.

Back at the Black residence, the children's lessons were coming along well. Cheri and Matt had learned to hate the Red's, as their new belief systems, had been placed inside their heads. The final thing that they would learn would cause them sleepless nights; as a matter of fact, in the future, it would cause them many fights!

Mr. and Mrs. Black took their children to see the sacred place. It was the very spot the disaster occurred, which changed, the entire ant race. A large colony of black ants had lived inside a town; then one day it happened, the Gods just tore it down. Everyone perished in the blink of an eye, there was nothing left standing, and the children wanted to know why!

To their horror, the answer was impossible to ignore! "Because" said Mr. Black, "the ants in this town, cut the Reds far too much slack. They let the Reds live next door, which upset the Gods and made them sore. The Gods had no choice, but to crush this passive voice! And now you know what happens, to those who like the Reds, don't you ever talk to them, or the Gods will have your heads!"

Back at the Red residence, the children's lessons were coming along well. Ron and Sal had learned to hate the Blacks, as their new belief system was taught with scary facts. The final thing that they would learn would cause them sleepless nights; as a matter of fact, in the future, it would cause them many fights!

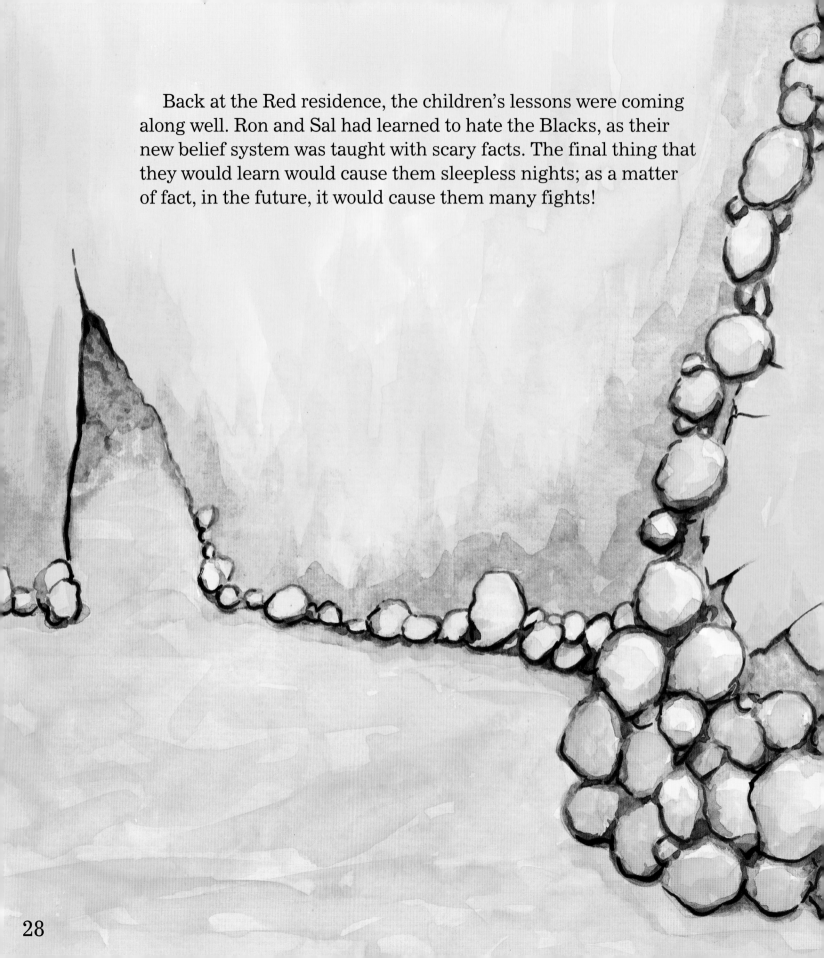

Mr. and Mrs. Red took their children to see the sacred place. It was the very spot the disaster occurred, which changed, the entire ant race. A large colony of red ants had lived inside a town; then one day it happened, the Gods just tore it down. Everyone perished in the blink of an eye, there was nothing left standing, and the children wanted to know why!

To their horror, the answer was impossible to ignore. "Because" said Mr. Red, "the Ants in this town, cut the Blacks far too much slack. They let the Blacks live next door, which made the Gods mad and sore. The Gods had no choice, but to crush this passive voice! And now you know what happens, to those who like the Blacks, don't you ever talk to them, or the Gods will turn their backs!"

Terry and Swan had been on the sea for a very long time. They had long since forgiven themselves, for their fateful climb. They turned their attention to the moment at hand, and that brought them peace, as they traveled to a new land.

Let's stop the story for a moment or two;
there are a few things about life,
that I would like to explain to you.

When we live in this moment, and that means the present... we can't live in the future, that hasn't been sent... we can't live in the past... that happened the moment before last.

We live right here and right now, and by the way that is the only time we can experience our life... Always Now... In This Moment.

Now... back to the story!

The boat came to a sudden stop, and Terry and Swan peeked over the top. To their surprise and joy, they could see land, and something very familiar, a beach full of sand! "Yea," they cried, as they jumped up and down, where there was land, there was sure be a town! They got off the boat as fast as you please; they had had enough of the wide-open seas.

Now one thing that ants have that really serves them well, is their ability to find other ants, where they live and dwell. The Blues used their senses to lead them to others; and whom did they find? Of course, the Black and Red sisters and brothers.

There they all were and ready to fight, both sides believed that their truth was right. They believed in the stories, which they had been told, stories that were actually hundreds of years old!

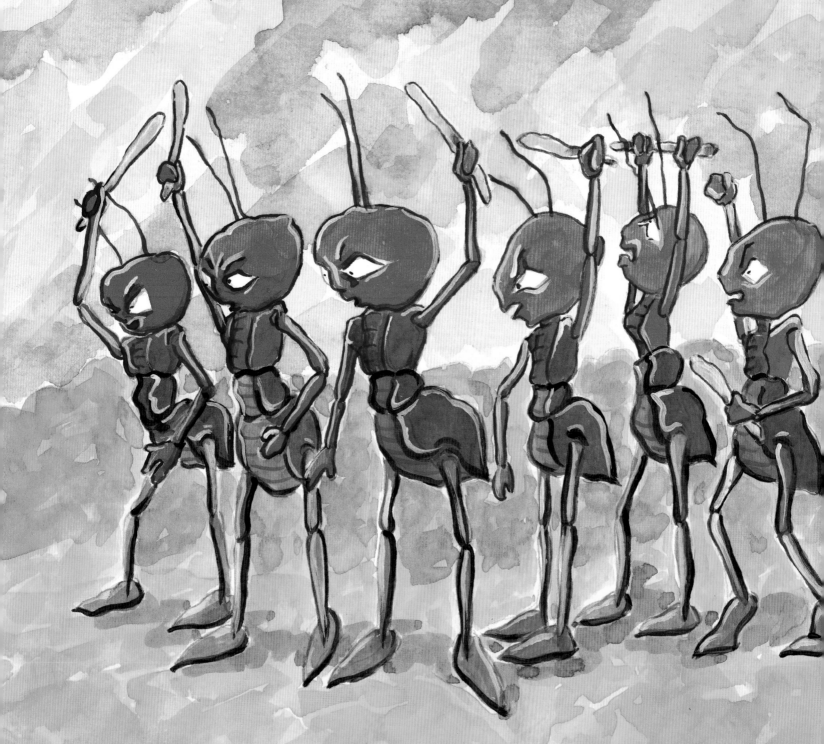

When Cheri and Matt, spotted Terry and Swan, they thought they were Blacks, and yelled, "Hey, come-on!"

At the very same time, Sal and Ron saw them too; they thought they were Reds, and yelled, "Come over, both of you!"

In that moment, the Blue's had no idea what to do, so they turned to the only thing that they really knew. Acceptance of all was what they had been taught, and they put that to use, believe it or not! They stepped in the middle of all of the fuss, and asked all their peers, to stop and discuss.

"What is the problem," Swan asked the group, and that's when the Blues, learned the entire scoop.

Shocked and amazed at the story they heard, they asked all their peers if they believed every word. "Yes," came the cry, from one and from all. "Everyone knows, the Gods want us to brawl!"

"Says who?" asked Terry, as he looked all around.

"Says the sacred place history," answered the group with resound.

"Oh...ummm... hmmm...we see the problem," said Terry and Swan, "Please listen up, and we'll help you move on."

In the next hour or so, the talk was intense, but for the Blacks and Reds it really made sense! The Blues gave all present, a different perspective, and the Blacks and the Reds became very reflective.

As Swan explained the loss of the town, she told of the many things that shared the same ground. "There are dogs and cats, soil and trees, humans and energy, water and bees. The list goes on forever," Swan said with a smile, "To think it was God… that isn't God's style! I'm sure it was an accident that leveled your towns, probably a bunch of humans that weigh many pounds!"

"The stories you've heard of the, 'Sacred Place', was the only explanation possible, for a prehistoric ant race. They passed it down, from one generation to another, and finally it was passed on, to your father and mother."

47

"Now that you know, that that myth was all wrong, it is your job to teach all ants, they belong! That brings us to the heart of the matter; it is time for us to help you, end your color chatter! When you saw us Blues, walking down the street, you thought we were your colors, and you wanted to meet. Please look at us closely, and see the colors we bear, you'll find we have common colors, of which we all share!"

In that instant the blinders were removed from the ants, and the laughter that followed became part of their chants. "We are brothers and sisters," they cried out with glee, "why didn't we know that, why couldn't we see?"

"Because," said Terry, as a matter of fact, "what you believed to be true, colored your view."

"As you can see now, we all share blue; in fact, that is the biggest part, of all of our hue! Since you changed your beliefs, which is easy to do, your perception has changed, which allows a new view!"

From that moment on, the ants started teaching their new
truth! And to think it all happened, by a chance meeting of youth!

And now for You! Before you go, there are a few things
the Ants and I would like you to know.

You are a Great Gift to the World!

You are Loved every second of every day!

You are One with everything there is!

We are looking forward to seeing you soon.
Thank you for reading, "Our Story!"

The Beginning

HELLO, MY NAME IS BRIAN, AND I WANTED TO SHARE A PERSONAL MESSAGE WITH YOU. THE FLAG AND SYMBOL THAT YOU SEE ON THE NEXT PAGE IS YOURS! WHEN YOU SEE IT FLYING IN THE WIND OR DISPLAYED ON SOMEONE'S CLOTHING, JUST KNOW THAT ITS PURPOSE IS TO REMIND YOU OF YOUR CONNECTION WITH EVERYONE AND EVERYTHING.

I WANT YOU TO KNOW THAT YOU MAKE A DIFFERENCE IN OUR WORLD. IF EVER YOU WONDER WHY YOU ARE HERE, JUST REMEMBER THAT YOU HAVE THE ANSWER INSIDE OF YOU. THANK YOU FOR WHO YOU ARE!

YOU ARE LOVED VERY, VERY, VERY,

MUCH!!!

BRIAN ☺

The Universal Flag

This symbol was created through universal consciousness, in order to expand awareness.

The colors are vibrations of energy common to all.

The waves represent the ups and downs of daily life.

The gold band represents our highest teaching; Treat one another as you want to be treated.

The white represents the purity from which we come.

By displaying this symbol, we represent the truth of who we are...

We are, One with All...
We are, Divine Presence...
We are, Truth...
We are, Eternal...
We are, Interdependent on All...

These simple truths resonate deep within all of us.
The opportunity to spread *Truth*, rests with you...

To learn more about our Universal Flag, please visit us at:
www.UniversalFlag.org or call: 630-971-9391

"I'm smarter than you, because you're just a frog, why in the hierarchy of animals, you're really a clog!"

"I'm sorry," the frog said in reply, "I'm sure I'd be smarter, if I only could fly."

The conversation continued on in the very same way… unfortunately, it was always the same in each new day. After a time, and who could say how long, all frogs believed that they didn't belong.

It is not until a young group of tadpoles teach the birds and the frogs a higher Truth, that they are able to change their false beliefs, and learn to honor and respect one another.

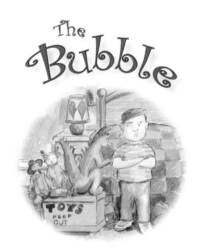

Once there was a little boy, who didn't want anyone to play with any of his toys…

As the little boy grows into a man, he only cares about his many material possessions. He meticulously cares for his things and keeps them only for himself. Because of his selfishness, one by one, the things he cares about most begin to leave his life. Soon he finds himself all alone, trapped inside a bubble.

"Oh no! came the cry, not salad again, wait until we grow up, we won't eat it then! "I hate fish," said Tom. "So do I," said Sue. "Why do we have to eat it? We wish we knew!"

Such was the talk in the Smith family that day, common to all, wouldn't you say? However, why is that so? And usually the same wherever we go?

We welcome you inside "our story," where you will rediscover the…secret of secrets!

the Raindrop

"I am just a raindrop,
I am smaller than small.
What am I doing here?
I have no use at all..."

So begins the story of the Raindrop. In this adventurous journey, many Truths are uncovered which help the Raindrop discover the higher purpose of its life.

the Sun and the Moon

It happened one day right out of the blue,
the Sun told the Moon he was tired and through.

"What do you mean?" the Moon asked the Sun,
"That would be the end of everything,
and that wouldn't be fun!"

The Sun and the Moon soon allow their fears to turn into anger. In that very instant, they walk out on their responsibilities, and cause unseen harm to the Earth and all who inhabit it. Eventually, the Sun and the Moon remember their interconnection with all, and quickly work together to restore balance.

The Up Down Day

"It was the craziest thing that I had ever seen...
I didn't know if I was awake, or just having a
dream! I turned on my lights to look at my
clock, and that's when I fell down in panic...
I was filled with shock."

"Everything that was down was no longer so.
Down was up and up was down...
it happened to everyone all over town!"

Who Am I?

"Who Am I?" came the cry.

"Don't You Know? mumbled my toe...

In this fun story, a young boy discovers a simple Truth from a most unusual group of teachers. As he looks beyond his Ego, he comes face to face with the reality of who he is.

One With All
Universal Flag